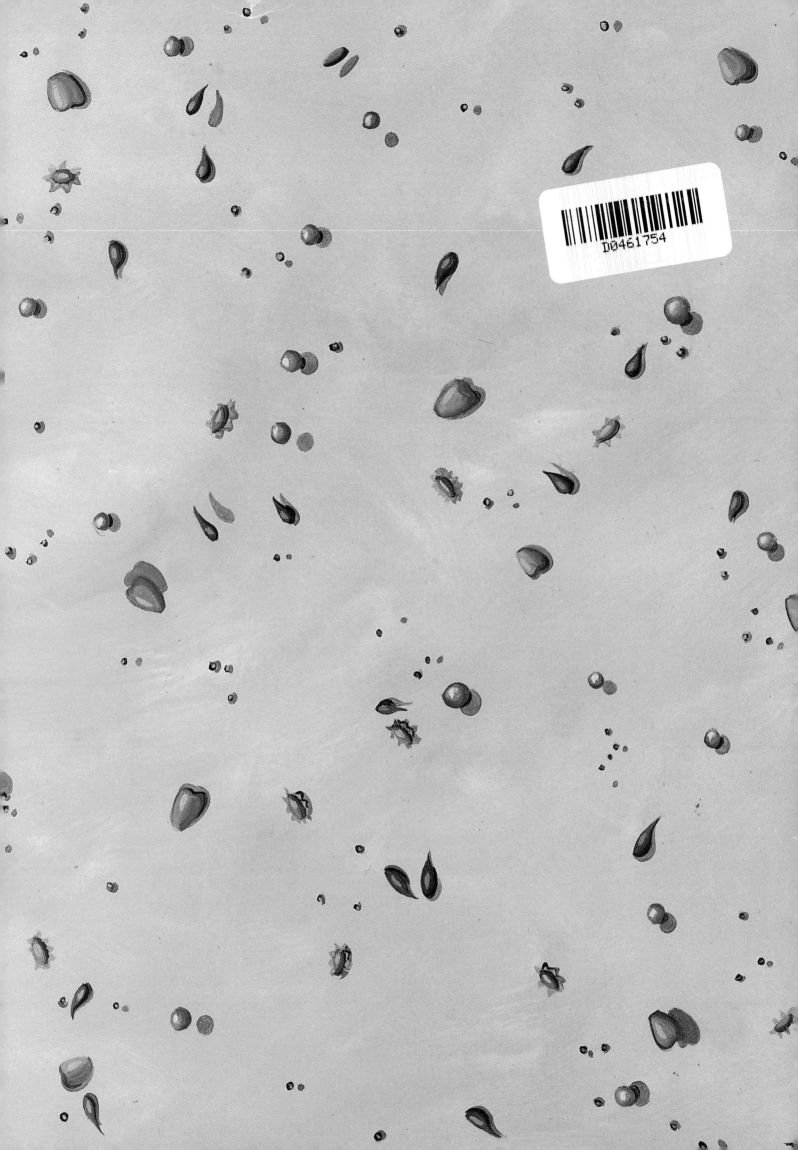

The Garden of Happiness

Written by Erika Tamar

Illustrated by Barbara Lambase

HARCOURT BRACE & COMPANY

San Diego   New York   London

Library of Congress Cataloging-in-Publication Data
Tamar, Erika.
The garden of happiness/by Erika Tamar; illustrated by Barbara Lambase.
p.   cm.
Summary: Marisol and her neighbors turn a vacant New York City lot
into a lush community garden.
ISBN 0-15-230582-3
[1. Community gardens—Fiction.   2. Gardens—Fiction.   3. City and
town life—Fiction.]   I. Lambase, Barbara, ill.   II. Title.
PZ7.T159Gar   1996
[E]—dc20   94-48836

F G E

Printed in Singapore

The paintings in this book were done in oil on Strathmore Illustration board.
The display type was hand-lettered by Georgia Deaver.
The text type was set in Goudy by Thompson Type, San Diego, California.
Color separations by Bright Arts Ltd., Singapore
Printed and bound by Tien Wah Press, Singapore
Production supervision by Warren Wallerstein and Ginger Boyer
Designed by Lori J. McThomas

For Monica
—E. T.

For John
—B. L.

On Marisol's block near East Houston Street, there was an empty lot that was filled with garbage and broken, tired things. It had a funky smell that made Marisol wrinkle her nose whenever she passed by.

One April morning, Marisol was surprised to see many grown-ups busy in the lot. Mr. Ortiz carried a rusty refrigerator door. Mrs. Willie Mae Washington picked up newspapers. Mr. Singh rolled a tire away.

The next afternoon, Marisol saw people digging up stones. Mr. Ortiz worked with a pickax.

"*¿Qué pasa?*" Marisol asked.

Mrs. Willie Mae Washington leaned on her shovel and wiped her forehead. "I'm gonna grow me black-eyed peas and greens and sweet potatoes, too," she said. "Like on my daddy's farm in Alabama. No more store-bought collard greens for me."

"We will call it The Garden of Happiness," Mr. Singh said. "I am planting *valore* — such a beautiful vine of lavender and red. Yes, everyone is happy when they see this bean from Bangladesh."

On another day, Marisol watched Mr. Castro preparing the ground. Mrs. Rodriguez rolled a wheelbarrow full of peat moss. Marisol inhaled the fresh-soil smell of spring.

"Oh, I want to plant something in The Garden of Happiness!" Marisol said.

"Too late, *niña*," Mr. Ortiz said. "All the plots are already taken."

Marisol looked everywhere for a leftover spot, but the ground was crisscrossed by markers of sticks and string. She looked and looked. Just outside the chain-link fence, she found a bit of earth where the sidewalk had cracked.

"¡*Mira!* Here's my patch!" Marisol called. It was no bigger than her hand, but it was her very own. She picked out the pebbles and scraped the soil with a stick.

Marisol noticed a crowd of teenagers across the street from the lot. They were staring at a brick wall. It was sad and closed up, without windows for eyes. Marisol crossed over to ask what they were doing.

"City Arts is giving us paint to make a mural on the wall," a girl told her.

"What will it be?" Marisol asked.

"Don't know yet," one of the big boys said. "We haven't decided."

"I'm making a garden," Marisol said. "I haven't decided, either, about what to plant."

In The Garden of Happiness, the ground had become soft and dark. Mr. Castro talked to his seedlings as he placed them in straight rows. "Come on now, little baby things, grow nice and big for me."

Marisol had no seedlings or even small cuttings or roots. *What can I do,*
she thought, *where can I find something to plant?*
    She went to the corner where old Mrs. Garcia was feeding the pigeons.

Marisol helped herself to a big flat seed. The birds fluttered about angrily. "Only one," she told them, "for my garden."

Marisol skipped back to her patch. She poked a hole with her finger, dropped in the seed, and patted the soil all around. And every single day that spring, Marisol carried a watering can to the lot and gave her seed a cool drink.

Before long, a green shoot broke through in Marisol's patch. Even on rainy days, she hurried to the lot to see. Soon there were two leaves on a strong, straight stalk, and then there were four. It became as high as Marisol's knee!

Green things were growing all around in The Garden of Happiness. Mr. Castro's tiny seedlings became big bushy things with ripe tomatoes shining like rubies.

"What's *my* plant?" Marisol asked. Now it reached to her shoulder. "What's it going to be?"

"Dunno," Mrs. Willie Mae Washington answered. "But it sure is *somethin'!*"

Marisol pulled out the weeds in the late afternoons, when it wasn't so summer-hot.

Sometimes she watched the teenagers across the street. They measured the wall. They talked and argued about what they would paint.

Often Marisol saw Mr. Ortiz in his plot, resting in a chair.

"I come back from the factory and breathe the fresh air," he said. "And I sit among my *habichuelas,* my little piece of Puerto Rico."

"Is *my* plant from Puerto Rico? Do you know what it is?" Marisol asked.

Mr. Ortiz shook his head and laughed. "*¡Muy grande!* Maybe it's Jack's beanstalk from the fairy tale."

By the end of July, Marisol's plant had grown way over her head. And then, at the very top, Marisol saw a bud! It became fatter every day. She couldn't wait for it to open.

"Now don't be lookin' so hard," Mrs. Willie Mae Washington chuckled. "It's gonna open up behind your back, just when you're thinkin' about somethin' else."

One morning, Marisol saw an amazing sight from halfway down the block. She ran the rest of the way. Standing higher than all the plants and vines in the garden was a flower as big as a plate! Her bud had turned into petals of yellow and gold.

"A sunflower!" Mrs. Anderson exclaimed as she pushed her shopping cart by. "Reminds me of when I was a girl in Kansas."

Mrs. Majewska was rushing on her way to the subway, but she skidded to a stop. "Ah, słoneczniki! So pretty in the fields of Poland!"

Old Mrs. Garcia shook her head. "No, no, *los girasoles* from Mexico, where they bring joy to the roadside."

"I guess sunflowers make themselves right at home in every sun-kissed place on earth," Mrs. Willie Mae Washington said.

"Even right here in New York City," Marisol said proudly.

The flower was a glowing circle, brighter than a yellow taxi. *A flower of sunshine*, Marisol thought, *the happiest plant in The Garden of Happiness.*

All summer long, it made the people on the street stop and smile.

Soon the air became cool and crisp with autumn. Mr. Castro picked the last of his tomatoes. Mr. Singh carried away a basket full of beans. Mrs. Rodriguez picked her *tomatillos*. "To dry and cut up for *salsa*," she said.

Mrs. Willie Mae Washington dug up orange potatoes. "I can almost smell my sweet potato pie." She winked at Marisol. "I'm gonna save an extra big slice for a good little gardener I know."

But something terrible was happening to Marisol's flower. Its leaves were turning brown and dry.

Marisol watered and watered until a stream ran down the sidewalk. But her flower's leaves began to fall.

"Please get well again," Marisol whispered.

Every day, more golden petals curled and faded.

"My flower of sunshine is sick," Marisol cried. "What should I do?"

"Oh, child," Mrs. Willie Mae Washington said. "Its season is over. There's a time to bloom and a time to die."

"No! I don't want my flower to die!"

"*Mi cariño,* don't cry," Mrs. Rodriguez said. "That's the way of a garden. You must save the seeds and plant again next spring."

Marisol's flower drooped to the ground. The Garden of Happiness wasn't happy for her anymore. The vines had tumbled down. The bushy green plants were gone. She collected the seeds and put them in her pocket, but spring was much too far away.

Marisol was too sad to go to the empty lot anymore. For a whole week, she couldn't even look down the block where her beautiful flower used to be.

Then one day she heard people calling her name.
"Marisol! Come quick!"
"Marisol! *¡Apúrate!* Hurry!"

A golden haze shone on the street. There was a big crowd, like on a holiday. Music from the *bodega* was loud and bright. And what she saw made Marisol laugh and dance and clap her hands.

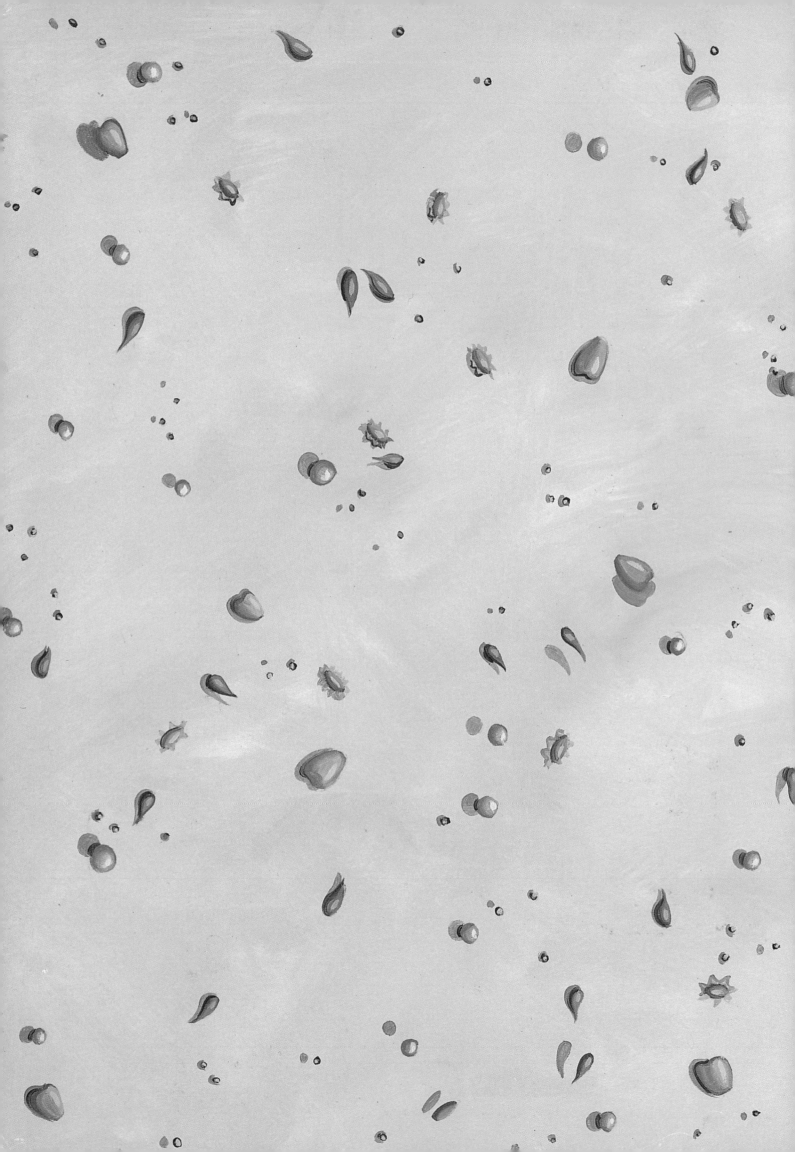